Also by Eileen Moore

The Dark at the Foot of the Stairs

For older readers

The Ghost Watchers

A Perfect
Fright

A Perfect Fright

Eileen Moore

Illustrated by Moira Kemp

h

Hodder
Children's
Books

CHAPTER ONE

"What is Mr Flanagan's ghost train really like?" Mickey Niff asked Tommy Cotton as they walked back from school. From his bedroom window, Tommy Cotton could see the fairground. At night, the fairground seemed like a small town filled with strange buildings. The ghost train was the strangest building of all.

"Go and see for yourself," Tommy Cotton said, mysteriously.

Mr Flanagan's ghost train was the scariest, the most frightening ride ever invented. Everyone who took a ride was awarded a ghost-train badge.

Tommy Cotton knew that Mickey Niff badly wanted a badge like the one fixed firmly onto his own bag. After Tommy had plucked up the courage to go there at last, he was determined to keep all the terrifying secrets of the ride to himself.

Mickey Niff drew in a deep and noisy breath, and ran his fingers through his dark, unruly hair. He was staying with Tommy Cotton who lived with his grandma, and they were walking to Grandma Cotton's house together. Their school bags were heavy with books and football boots, so they each leaned to one side, matching, except for Tommy Cotton's pale and spikey hair. Mickey Niff swung his bag to his other shoulder and leaned to the other side. If only he dared ride on the ghost train too!

The famous ghost train had certainly scared Tommy Cotton. Inside, each nook and cranny hid the weirdest kind of creatures that only Mr Flanagan could ever imagine. Every night since he had taken the ride, Tommy would lie his freckled face against the carpet to explore the space under his bed. He would look warily around every corner and search inside every cupboard before he closed his eyes. Although he would certainly have been surprised to find a witch crouching there, he was never quite sure that the cupboard would be completely empty.

Grandma Cotton was different. At night, she would turn off the lights in the house making a musical sound of sharp clicks, before striding fearlessly through the darkness and up the stairs. She would reach her bed easily, out of habit, and know without the slightest doubt there would be nothing at all to lurk between the carpet and the mattress. Then, she would close her eyes with a snap and sleep deeply until morning. She would lie thin and undreaming under the brightly coloured covers, her knees and upturned toes making small mounds under the duvet, like chunks of apples hidden in a pie.

When Tommy Cotton arrived home with Mickey Niff, he found Grandma Cotton quivering with excitement.

"Whatever's the matter?" he asked,
dropping his bag on the floor. "Has
something happened?" He noticed that
Grandma Cotton had been to the
fairground again because there was a new
coconut, not yet dusty, on the shelf.

Grandma Cotton loved the fairground.
The kitchen was partly furnished with
goldfish swimming in their bowls, and
garnished with coconuts. The curtains and
cushions were coloured bright orange to
match the goldfish, and the matting on the

floor might have been woven from the coconut's straggly beards.

The Mad Demon Ride was Grandma Cotton's favourite. A rollercoaster of the most breathtaking dives and whirls, it scared her more than a dead rat's skull. Strangely, the ghost train did not scare her one jot. She had remarked upon this, rather proudly, although mistakenly, to Mr Flanagan. She had told him that the ghost train made her laugh!

But just then, Grandma Cotton had the most exciting news. She fastened her fingers tightly around a potato-peeler to make the afternoon seem ordinary.

"Sit down!" she said in a wavering voice, "and listen!" Tommy Cotton sat down at the table and so did Mickey Niff. Grandma Cotton released the potato-peeler and held the edge of the table with both hands. She was small, and thin and wiry, and looked as though she might easily break into pieces.

"Mr Flanagan is taking a holiday" she said,

breathlessly. "He has asked me
if I will take charge of the ghost train!"

Mickey Niff stared. His eyes seemed big
and round as ginger nuts.

"There's no need to look like that,
Mickey Niff," Grandma Cotton told him,
briskly, and added, "you'll both need to
help me look after the ghost train until Mr
Flanagan comes back. The track'll need
oiling and all the bony skeletons and weird
witches'll need dusting."

"There's horrible cobwebs dangling and

13

trailing everywhere," Tommy Cotton murmured, shivering.

"Nonsense," Grandma Cotton said, firmly. "They'll only be old and grimy dishcloths torn into shreds and hanging there. I've no doubt Mrs Flanagan saves them especially."

Grandma Cotton looked around. The kitchen door had been flung open. Mickey Niff had gone!

Down the street, Tommy Cotton caught up with Mickey Niff.

"The ghost train's only a fairground ride," he reasoned, sensibly. "There can't be anything really horrible there at all. Everything inside only seems horrible because of the pitch darkness."

Mickey Niff looked sulky. "You were scared out of your wits though," he argued.

Tommy Cotton glanced at Mickey Niff. "That was last year," he said, as though he had grown several years older since then. "I can see now that even the most horrible witch is only one of Mr Flanagan's models."

Mr Flanagan had built the ghost train himself, taking years. Even when he was only eight years old, the ghost train had begun to take shape in his mind. He had

brooded, and had rattled his brains, upon
how best he could frighten people. His
workshop, filled with secrets, was kept
locked.

Mickey Niff said he could hardly walk
past the ghost train without suffering a
dreadful attack of asthma. "There might
be haunted ghost trains," he said,
suddenly. "In a ghost train, a real ghost
could terrify people, and no one would
know there was a real ghost."

Tommy Cotton looked sideways at Mickey Niff.

"You do have weird ideas," he said.

Mickey Niff stopped and leaned against a fence. "What are real ghosts for anyway?" he asked. "What do real ghosts do best?"

Tommy Cotton looked thoughtful. He shrugged. "Scare people, I suppose."

"That's exactly right," Mickey Niff agreed, "and they can scare people best in a ghost train. No one would ever know the difference, especially in Mr Flanagan's ghost train. No one would ever suspect a real ghost."

They turned to go back.

"What is inside?" Mickey Niff asked again.

"There'll be lights in the ghost train. Mr Flanagan'll have fitted lights. We'll go when the fairground's closed. Then you can see

17

everything with the lights turned on. You'll
see all the skeletons and ghosts, and the
horrible witches. You'll see they're only
made of plastic, and bundles of rags."

Mickey Niff began to look cheerful.

"We could make the ghost train into a
den, so long as there are lights," Tommy
Cotton added, excitedly. He began to
imagine how they would have the most
wonderful time, riding in the trucks when
the fairground was closed. They would have
the most marvellous den in the world.

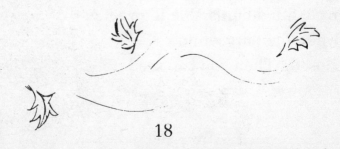

CHAPTER TWO

At that moment, rather surprisingly, Mr
Flanagan was in his house. He had only
pretended to be taking a holiday. Instead,
he was sitting quietly and devising a
cunning plan. The trouble was that he kept
on remembering Grandma Cotton, the only
person who had ever ridden in the ghost
train and not been terrified, the only person
to laugh at the ghost train.

"That's only one person in
years and years,"
Mrs Flanagan told
him, soothingly. But
still Mr Flanagan
looked glum and
gloomy.

He brooded. For days, he stared at the
wallpaper. He simply could not rest.
He felt that he had failed.

"You must find a way to frighten
Grandma Cotton," Mrs Flanagan
said, speaking practically .
"Then you're *bound*
to feel better, dear."

So, Mr Flanagan cheered up enormously. Soon, his plan began to take shape. So long as he could frighten Grandma Cotton, he would feel better. First, he pretended to go on holiday. For his plan to succeed, he needed Grandma Cotton to be in charge of the fantastic ghost train. Then, he would set to work to make the most terrifying and dreadful witch imaginable! A witch that would send Grandma Cotton fleeing for her life!

The next day, Grandma Cotton began work at the fairground. Before she left home, she wondered if she should wear her gloomy clothes; a long, black, rustling skirt, and a silky grey blouse with wide and billowing sleeves. These smelt delicately of moth balls. Her grey hair, usually fastened with a neat clip, she left tangled, uncombed and unpinned, to catch the mood of Mr Flanagan's cobwebs.

"That's far too grisly," Tommy Cotton remarked, heaping jam onto the steaming porridge. "Go looking bright and cheerful. Then, inside, the ghost train will seem even more horrible."

"Yes," Mickey Niff agreed, wide-eyed and nodding vigorously.

Grandma Cotton frowned slightly.

"I have heard," she said, looking at herself sideways through the mirror, "that Mrs Flanagan often makes herself useful in the ghost train, adding to the mood of the place. She has been known to haunt the ghost train for hours, adding a particularly life-like touch."

Grandma Cotton was right. Mr Flanagan was forever grateful to his wife. It was whispered that he had chosen to marry her for exactly this reason, only pretending that he had fallen in love. Grandma Cotton peered into the mirror. There was not a single wart. Clearly, she could not match the raging success of Mrs Flanagan.

"You're right!" she agreed, and changed

into cheerful clothes, her face tinged pink with excitement.

In the kitchen, Tommy Cotton and Mickey Niff were almost ready for school.

"Come to the fairground if you like on the way home," Grandma Cotton said, opening the door and laying a patch of sunshine onto the floor.

"All right," Tommy Cotton said, wondering if he could persuade Mickey Niff to go there too. Grandma Cotton took hold of the bicycle that leaned against the wall. A dandelion was tangled in the spokes. Tommy Cotton stood on the doorstep. "Good luck!" he called out as he watched Grandma Cotton ride away. The bicycle looked cheerful wearing the dandelion.

On the way to school, Tommy Cotton said, "You will come to the fairground with me, won't you? You don't still mind about the ghost train, do you?" Mickey Niff frowned deeply. "I'm not sure," he said, thoughtfully. "It's because of my asthma. I might not mind standing outside now."

"You can't have asthma just because of a ghost train," Tommy Cotton said, reasonably, "not even Mr Flanagan's ghost train."

"I can," Mickey Niff said. They walked on.

"Come anyway," Tommy Cotton said. He would turn on the lights when the ghost train was closed. Mickey Niff would see there was nothing there, only a fantastic display of tricks and illusions. He couldn't wait to see everything for himself. They would have the most marvellous time.

"We'll keep the ghost train a secret though," he told Mickey Niff, "just you and me."

"That's right," Mickey Niff agreed, breathlessly, "no one else."

CHAPTER THREE

After school, Tommy Cotton and Mickey
Niff walked to the fairground. There was a
long queue for the ghost train.

"You see," Tommy Cotton told Mickey
Niff, "it's only a fairground ride," but he
shivered. Mickey Niff looked solemn and
shifted uneasily. He made an effort to fix
his mind on Mrs Flanagan's dishcloths.

"We'll be able to look inside soon,"
Tommy Cotton said, enthusiastically. "Let's
have a look at the rest of the fairground and
come back here at closing time."

"I'd like a hot dog," Mickey Niff said.
They wandered from stall to stall and
bought hot dogs.

"I think I should tell you now," Mickey

Niff said, firmly, "I'm not riding on that
ghost train in the dark." They were passing
a spectacular merry-go-round. The golden
horses rose and fell beside them. Tommy
Cotton paused. Perhaps he would never be
able to persuade Mickey Niff to go inside,
even under the bright lights. There was no
point in having such an extraordinary and
wonderful den if he could only go there by
himself. He wondered too, if Mr Flanagan's
ghost train would seem so appealing even in
bright lights, to anyone sitting there alone,

next to a witch that might look surprisingly like Mrs Flanagan.

"All right," Tommy Cotton shouted above the sound of the organ music that came from the roundabouts, "only when the light's are on." Even though he could hardly imagine lights in such a liquorice kind of darkness, only the grey, eerie lights that lit the weird sights and made the shadows there.

At closing time, there was no doubt that Grandma Cotton was very tired. Her arms dangled loosely beside her, rather in the style of Mr Flanagan's cobwebs. Her hair trailed too, in wisps.

"Ah! There you are!" Grandma Cotton held out a key on a huge iron ring. The key certainly matched the ghost train, the kind of key that would open the door of a haunted castle, or a prison cell. Mr Flanagan was devoted to detail. The key was long and thin, like a witch's finger.

"Take this key
and lock the
ghost train before
you leave,"
Grandma Cotton
said, rather wearily.
She picked up her
belongings. The key was labelled,
Ghost Train. Tommy Cotton's eyes glowed.
The key felt cold in his hands. Perhaps no
one had ever touched the ghost-train key
before, besides Grandma Cotton, except
Mr Flanagan, of course.

Grandma Cotton picked up the bicycle
and began to wobble away, waving without
looking back. Suddenly, Mickey Niff
grinned. No one could feel terrified under
bright lights, he told himself. It was only
the darkness that made everything seem so
terrible. He began to feel excited. Soon
there would be a ghost-train badge pinned
to his school bag, without the dreadful

nuisance of Tommy Cotton's nightmares happening to him.

The trouble began with an unexpected muddle that caused the most dreadful catastrophe. No one was really to blame.

"Well, muddles do happen," Grandma Cotton said, afterwards. And there was no doubt that a muddle had happened, quite unexpectedly. Even before Grandma Cotton had ridden out of sight, Tommy Cotton jumped into the first of the trucks that faced the black, tightly fitting doors.

"Come on!" he shouted, excitedly to Mickey Niff. "There's room for both of us!"

"What I'd like to know is," Mickey Niff explained, folding his arms and not budging, "did Grandma Cotton switch on the lights in the ghost train before she left? Or is it still dark inside there?" They both stared at the thick, heavy doors. There was not a chink of light or darkness to give any clue. Tommy Cotton hesitated.

He thought that he should be the one to take charge, because of belonging to Grandma Cotton, so he said, "You come and sit here, Mickey Niff, and I'll investigate." Just then, no one suspected that such an amazing muddle was about to happen. Mickey Niff and Tommy Cotton changed places.

Tommy Cotton searched everywhere for the switches. There was only one, which was pointing upwards. Tommy Cotton gazed thoughtfully at the switch. He knew that usually, switches pointing upwards are turned off, and those pointing downwards are turned on.

"Good thinking, Mickey Niff," he remarked, thankfully. The lights were turned off. He shivered when he thought that the trucks might have raced forward into utter blackness, instead of into their new and brightly lit den. Tommy Cotton clicked down the switch. That was the

beginning of the muddle,
because Tommy Cotton
had made the worst
possible mistake.

He had clicked the
switch that started the ghost-
train truck, the same switch
that operated every piece of winding
machinery inside, and not the light switch.
Beyond the heavy black doors, ghosts in
grey shadows began to drift.

The truck glided silently along the
track, carrying Mickey Niff slowly forward.
He looked puzzled as he sat alone in the
truck. He could not imagine why he was
moving further and further away from
Tommy Cotton, who thought there was
no point in making matters worse by
looking miserable. Instead, Tommy
Cotton, looking fairly bright, smiled
encouragingly at Mickey
Niff, as though

no muddle at all had happened.

Mickey Niff held on tightly, white-knuckled as the truck gathered speed to plunge forward at an amazing pace. He opened his eyes wide, drawing in a long, deep breath. The truck raced towards the doors which snapped open to devour the truck and Mickey Niff. In an instant, Mickey Niff was gone. The doors closed after him, tight as a crocodile's jaws.

Tommy Cotton waited. He dug the end of his trainers into the damp earth under his feet. The fairground was an eerie, silent place. He could hear nothing. He had seen Mickey Niff turn the nasty pale colour of a potato, a peeled potato too. He looked towards the doors and wondered if he should jump into the next truck to follow Mickey Niff inside. The sky was turning dark. The trouble was that Mickey Niff was just not the right kind of person to be emptied into Mr Flanagan's ghost train . Mickey Niff was the right kind of person to be emptied *out* of the ghost train, as quickly as possible, Tommy Cotton thought. So, he waited.

Tommy Cotton waited for a long time. Mr Flanagan believed in taking time for frightening people. Although the trucks careered forward at an alarming rate, many of Mr Flanagan's ghastly inventions loomed out of the darkness fairly slowly, beginning

only as faint and silent shadows. After all,
Mr Flanagan always reasoned, he had spent
years in concocting the ghost train. He was
anxious that people should be truly terrified
before emerging from such grisly depths.
He intended that no detail of his dreadful
masterpiece should be missed. Once
people were trapped inside the ghost
train, Mr Flanagan did not like
anyone to escape too soon.

Meanwhile, outside the
ghost train was
proving fairly
terrifying too.

In the creepy kind of moonlight, Tommy Cotton could hear footsteps. Every second, the footsteps drew nearer and nearer. Tommy Cotton's heart raced faster than a ghost train truck. Dreadful thoughts came into his head. Perhaps, in the darkness, when the fairground was empty and closed, Mr Flanagan's horrible inventions drifted from the ghost train into the cool night air.

At night, the ghosts and witches, like Grandma Cotton, had finished their work. Why should they stay inside, Tommy Cotton reasoned, when outside, there was darkness too? Tommy Cotton dared not look around. The footsteps came nearer and nearer.

CHAPTER FOUR

Earlier that day, Mr Gumtree, the Science
Master at Tommy Cotton's school, had been
selling raffle-tickets for the
Model Railway Society on
which he was keen. He
had stacked the tickets in a
neat pile on his desk, smiled
his skipping rope- shaped smile
and wondered, rather craftily, if he could
persuade the class to take away the stack
and sell it to their aunties and
grandmothers. His own aunties and
grandmothers were rather thin on the
ground, so he had made the Science
lesson as interesting as possible that day,
and had even suggested an irresponsible but

excellent recipe for gunpowder.

Tommy Cotton, whose thoughts on gunpowder were only overshadowed by his thoughts on fairgrounds and ghost trains, had left the raffle-tickets on his desk, by mistake.

"No matter," Mr Gumtree said to himself, rather huffily. He would take the raffle-tickets to Grandma Cotton. After all, Tommy Cotton's house was on his way home. He remembered that once, he had found Grandma Cotton on the doorstep, polishing the doorknob. He had stopped for a chat, and quite unexpectedly, Grandma Cotton had invited him inside to drink tea and to sample her warm jam tarts. When Mr Gumtree thought of the jam tarts, he was remarkably pleased and no longer huffy. He put on his coat, picked up the tickets, and strode out of school. Not long afterwards, Mr Gumtree reached Tommy Cotton's house.

The door bell was swaying in the wind, at the end of a loose wire, like a flower at the end of a stem, and was hard to catch.

So Mr Gumtree knocked on the door instead of ringing the bell. Rather limply and droopily, Grandma Cotton opened the door. She was even more tired after riding her bicycle home from the fairground.

"Oh, Mr Gumtree, please come in," she said, wondering what Tommy Cotton had been doing, and expecting the worst. Mr Gumtree strode over the doorstep and sat down heavily in an armchair. There was a warm stripe down the middle of the armchair and a very narrow warm patch on each arm.

"What brings you here?" Grandma Cotton asked, sitting down in a different chair.

Mr Gumtree's head was filled with jam tarts and raffle-tickets, so he said, by mistake, "I've come to leave some jam tarts for Tommy Cotton to sell. They're here in my pocket."

"That's no use," Grandma Cotton remarked. "There's too many jam tarts here already. That tin is filled with them." She nodded towards a nearby shelf and added, "Strawberry and apricot." She thought that any jam tarts crammed in Mr Gumtree's pocket would be distressingly crummy.

Mr Gumtree shifted uneasily, but being a school teacher, he had a remarkable brain. Thinking quickly, he said,

"Well, how very kind, Grandma Cotton, I'd be delighted." He passed the tin to her, so that she could offer him one or two. Then, rather munchily and crumbily, while drinking a cup of tea to match, Mr Gumtree explained that he had really meant raffle-tickets and not jam tarts at all.

"Where's Tommy Cotton?" he asked, suddenly.

"Tommy Cotton's at the fairground," Grandma Cotton explained, rather anxiously, glancing at the clock that was ticking loudly on the wall.

"Isn't the fairground closed now?" Mr Gumtree asked, surprised. So Grandma Cotton told him, excitedly, about how she had been left in charge of Mr Flanagan's ghost train. "Of course, the fairground's closed now," she explained, almost breathlessly, "Tommy Cotton's locking the ghost train doors for me and then walking home."

"Mr Flanagan's ghost train?" Mr Gumtree said, raising his eyebrows, and making wrinkles appear everywhere on his forehead, like train lines at a busy railway station. "That ghost train ought to be banned. I've heard that it's far too terrifying for children. Where's Mickey Niff?"

"He's with Tommy Cotton," Grandma Cotton said. She leaned forward and added, agreeably, "Now Mickey Niff will certainly have bad dreams for a fortnight after a ride on Mr Flanagan's ghost train."

Mr Gumtree fastened the last escaped crumbs onto his damp finger before whisking them away. He stood up.

"If you like, Grandma Cotton," he said, "I'll go back that way and hurry Tommy Cotton along. It'll be no trouble."

"And Mickey Niff," Grandma Cotton said, gratefully, sinking into the completely warm armchair.

"And Mickey Niff," Mr Gumtree agreed, cheerfully. He always enjoyed hurrying children along. He left the raffle-tickets on the table and said goodbye.

CHAPTER FIVE

At the fairground, Tommy Cotton's eyes grew wider and wider. The footsteps drew closer and closer. A black shape loomed out of the darkness.

"Ah! There you are, Tommy!" Tommy Cotton breathed a loud sigh of relief. The black shape was only Mr Gumtree after all.

"I told Grandma Cotton I'd hurry you along," Mr Gumtree explained.

"I'm waiting for Mickey Niff," Tommy Cotton said. "He's disappeared inside the ghost train, by mistake."

"By mistake?" Mr Gumtree sounded surprised.

"I pressed the wrong switch," Tommy Cotton said, looking downcast. "Mickey Niff's been inside for ages and ages."

Mr Gumtree stepped backwards and, leaning to one side in the style of a bent lamp-post, gazed along the outer walls to study the exact size of Mr Flanagan's great invention.

"That ghost train's not so big," he said. "I've no doubt those trucks move around on tracks shaped like a Catherine Wheel on firework night, or move up and down in stripes like a lawn mower. That's why the ghost train seems such a long ride." He paused, then added, "Perhaps Mickey Niff's truck has broken down."

"I can't find the light switch," Tommy Cotton said, unhappily.

"No need for lights," Mr Gumtree said, cheerfully climbing into the next truck. "Ghost trains don't scare me one jot. If you can find the right switch to start this truck, Tommy Cotton, I'll go inside and investigate."

Tommy Cotton was only too pleased to agree. He was glad Mr Gumtree had arrived to help find Mickey Niff.

He pressed the switch at once. A moment later, Mr Gumtree zoomed away like a rocket and was soon out of sight.

Mr Gumtree had hardly vanished when Mickey Niff made a spectacular reappearance. The truck rattled to a halt. Tommy Cotton feared the worst. He was relieved to see there was no sign of Mickey Niff's asthma. Instead, Mickey Niff stared straight ahead. He wore a strange expression, and breathed rather quickly as though he had been running a race.

At first, Tommy Cotton thought he would say he was very sorry for sending Mickey Niff on such a disastrous journey.

But then, He quickly changed his mind. He decided to stay cheerful instead, as though he didn't expect Mickey Niff to mind the ghastly frights of Mr Flanagan's ghost train.

Mickey Niff climbed slowly out of the truck, still breathing heavily and still saying nothing. He looked different.

"Ah! There you are! Now wasn't that a stupendous ride?" Tommy Cotton remarked encouragingly, as though Mickey Niff had joined the queue earlier in the day, and as though there had been no muddle at all. Mickey Niff didn't answer. He stared ahead as though he had not heard a single word, so Tommy Cotton added in quite an ordinary kind of way, "Mr Gumtree is having a ride too," as though Mr Gumtree was at that moment, drifting by on a golden horse and not in a truck in the gruesome ghost train. "We'll wait for Mr Gumtree. Then we can lock the doors and go home."

Mickey Niff still wore a dreamy look, no

doubt a nightmare kind of dream, Tommy Cotton thought, uneasily. Perhaps the first nightmare was beginning to form, even before Mickey Niff had a chance to fall asleep.

Ages afterwards, when Mickey Niff had still not said one word, Mr Gumtree was finally spilled out of the ghost train. There was no doubt he was worse than hot and bothered. He struggled out of the truck even before it had come to a halt, but kept his eyes fixed on the doors through which he had just crashed, as though making sure that an eerie and terrifying fiend was not chasing him.

"Ah, you've come back!" Tommy Cotton said. Mr Gumtree was the colour of a fresh mackerel, although this was difficult to see in the moonlight. He took a large red handkerchief

49

and wiped his shiny head which, Tommy
Cotton imagined, had been similarly
polished with Mrs Flanagan's trailing
dishcloths. Mr Gumtree shuddered.

"Of course I've come back!" he gasped,
in a dithering voice. "Where's Mickey Niff?"
and he peered into the darkness.

"He's here," Tommy Cotton said. "He
isn't talking."

Mr Gumtree moved shakily away from
the ghost train and steadied himself for a
moment against the hot dog stall. There
was still the comforting aroma of hot dogs,
even though these were quite cold and
locked away.

"Mickey Niff's in a dreadful state of
shock," Mr Gumtree said. "This wretched
ghost train's given him the fright of his life!"
Tommy Cotton felt sorry to hear this.
Mickey Niff might take days to recover, and
might never go into the ghost train again,
not even when there were lights. Mr

Gumtree was more than flustered too. He glanced towards the doors again, and almost shouted, "The key, Tommy Cotton! Lock those doors at once!"

Tommy Cotton poked the long, thin key into the door lock. The shutters unfolded and locked away the trucks. "You'll need to take Mickey Niff home right away," Mr Gumtree said, his voice still quivering to match the rest of him which was shivering. "It's a very cold night," he added, just so that Tommy Cotton and Mickey Niff would not suspect that he had been scared out of his wits too.

They all hurried away from the fairground. Mr Gumtree wished his head could be filled with raffle-tickets and warm jam tarts. But there were only ghosts and skeletons instead.

At last, when Tommy Cotton and Mickey Niff were sitting inside Grandma Cotton's warm and brightly lit kitchen, Grandma

Cotton poured out two enormous bowls of soup. She listened while Tommy Cotton explained how he had sent Mickey Niff into the ghost train by mistake. She glanced at Mickey Niff and said, briskly,

"Eat that up, Mickey Niff. You'll be as right as rain in no time."

Mickey Niff picked up the spoon in front of him, took a mouthful of hot soup, and asked, "Can I have a ghost-train badge?"

CHAPTER SIX

The next day at school,
Mickey Niff proudly wore his
ghost-train badge.

Everyone gathered
around and he felt more
brave than he had ever
felt before.

In the classroom, Mr
Gumtree looked stern and
serious. He looked gloomy too.

"Sit down, everyone," he ordered, "I
have something important to say."

Everyone sat down. They could tell that
Mr Gumtree was going to make a special
announcement.

"Today," Mr Gumtree began, clearing

his throat, "I would like to tell you of the horrible consequences and dangers of taking a ride in Mr Flanagan's ghost train."

There was complete silence, so Mr Gumtree continued. "Yesterday, I decided to inspect the ghost train for myself and I must say that it is the most terrifying ride ever found on a fairground." Mr Gumtree had not slept well. Ghosts, not jam tarts, still drifted through his thoughts. He shuddered, remembering. "I expect anyone riding in Mr Flanagan's ghost train will have bad dreams for a month," he warned.

Tommy Cotton put up his hand and said, "Mr Flanagan has made a different kind of darkness there, a kind of blackness never seen before."

"That's right," Mr Gumtree agreed, and added, "Mr Flanagan has a horrible and nasty imagination. Those inventions make one's blood turn cold. That ghost train should be pulled down," Mr Gumtree narrowed his eyes for maximum effect. "I shall write to the Council," he added.

Harry Pickup, a small boy on the front row who wanted a ghost-train badge quite desperately, asked,

"But what *is* inside Mr Flanagan's ghost train?" Mr Gumtree cleared his throat.

"Witches!" he said, "Witches that scream and poke people, appear out of the pitch blackness, lit up with a horrible greyness. You can see every nasty wrinkle and wart, and every thin and twisted finger!"

"Witches with watery eyes and crooked noses," Tommy Cotton said, breathlessly, "and prowling black cats no one sees, only pairs of staring green eyes in the dark.

"Exactly," Mr Gumtree added, glancing at Tommy Cotton and grateful for the assistance. "There are terrifying ghosts, floating and moaning on all sides. The trucks go rattling on and there's no escape"

"What else?" murmured Harry Pickup, gazing intently at Mr Gumtree.

"Ghastly skeletons, uglier and bonier than anyone except Mr Flanagan could ever dream."

56

Harry Pickup still wanted a ghost train badge. Mr Gumtree could tell he did. So, Mr Gumtree, who was still worse than hot and bothered after the night before, lowered his voice almost to a whisper. He leaned forward and said, in a creepy kind of voice, "There's cobwebs trailing everywhere, and bats."

"How can people see bats in the dark?" Harry Pickup asked, still wanting a badge.

"You can see them black against the grey ghosts, as they flash by. Then they disappear and you can hear bones rattling and bats fluttering in the dark." Mr Gumtree took out a red and white spotted hanky and wiped his damp and shiny head.

"There's the haunted slime pond, and the ghoulish slug bog too," Tommy Cotton said, grimly.

Mr Gumtree turned to the comforting heap of science books in front of him.

"That's quite enough talk about Mr Flanagan's ghost train for today," he said, shakily. "I'm glad I inspected the ghost train myself, so that I could warn you all never to go there." He paused and attempted to look cheerful, but it seemed that he had left his skipping rope smile outside the ghost train and could still only look gloomy. "Now, please give out these books," he said.

But things did not go quite as Mr Gumtree intended. The moment break time came, there was pandemonium. All the people who were not wearing a ghost train badge, said they really must see the ghost train for themselves, especially the slime pondites and the slug boglins which no one had even dared to mention.

Everyone who had been before, remembered how horribly exciting they had found Mr Flanagan's ghost train and decided to go again. That day, after school, there was a long queue for the ghost train. Harry Pickup was the first.

On the way home, Tommy Cotton said to Mickey Niff,

"It's still only a fairground ride. Everything's still only made of plastic and junk, even if Mr Gumtree was scared out of his wits. Mr Flanagan's just marvellous at making special effects, and life-like models.

But Tommy Cotton was wrong. Really, everything was much, much more spooky!

Even at that very moment, Mr Flanagan was planning every detail of the most grisly and dreadful witch he had ever made. He would begin with Mrs Flanagan whom he noticed, had small, thin, wiry legs that could run fast, like a spider!

CHAPTER SEVEN

Mr Flanagan bent forward as he walked towards the fantastic workshop, his thick, long hair hiding his face. He was tall, and as thin as the key he held in his hand. Usually, he looked quite ordinary, but when he was intent upon ghosts and ghouls, his face twisted into a crooked smile. He wrung his hands together in a mischievous kind of way. His shoulders were hunched, and he crouched like a gnome.

Mr Flanagan thrust the long, narrow key into the lock, flung open the door, and stepped inside. A dim light filtered through a tiny window in the roof above his head. The light shone on the bottles and jars on the shelves that lined the walls. In the middle of the workshop, on a large and heavy table, small iron burners held flickering blue flames where curious coloured liquids curdled and bubbled and boiled.

Mr Flanagan peered into the glass jars and read the labels. Eyeballs, pickled like onions, floated and stared as he walked past. He came to the jar marked *Witches' Teeth*. The broken, spiky teeth were green, and brown and knarled as walnuts, and he dropped a handful

into his pocket, where they rattled as he walked. He reached for the jar above and took a fistful of *Hairy Warts* to add to those more usually worn by Mrs Flanagan.

"What next?" he murmured to himself, his eyes glinting wickedly. He reached for the *Horny Finger Nails*, and dropped the twistiest into his bag of *Wrinkles*, although no more wrinkles would fit onto Mrs Flanagan.

But, "Oh yes!" he told himself as he remembered. Mrs Flanagan would need a new snaky hairpiece, even

though her own hair was a
dream – a nightmare – being even
better than the tangled, knotty and straggly
wigs he kept in the boxes further away, next to
those marked *Crooked Noses*.

Enormous spiders rushed everywhere.
Anyone passing by activated the current that
controlled them. Of course, they were not
real. Neither were the bats. But next to the
box marked *Imitation Spiders All Sizes* was a large
cage labelled *Real Furry Ones*. In the darkness,
these spiders spun and hung the endless webs.

Mr Flanagan rummaged in the *Witches'*
Wardrobe where cloaks hung, black as beetles'
wings. He stuffed all that he needed into his
bag with a handful of *Poking Fingers* and
Liver Spots. Mrs Flanagan had her own tall hat
and broomstick which she kept under the
stairs, next to the vacuum cleaner and
the ironing board.

Oh! He almost forgot. He turned to the section marked *Noises* and took down tins of *Wails and Shrieks*

Afterwards, with a crafty smile, Mr Flanagan went outside and locked the door. Then, he sidled home to enjoy Mrs Flanagan's brew and stew. Mrs Flanagan dived excitedly into the bag, looking at everything, checking off the items as though these were pudding ingredients.

"You forgot the paraphernalia and stuff," she said, disappointedly, "and my favourite *Nasty Laugh*."

CHAPTER EIGHT

Grandma Cotton simply could not find the switch for the ghost-train lights. Every day, Tommy Cotton wanted to know if Grandma Cotton had found the switch. He could hardly wait to make the ghost train into his own fantastic den. No one in the world would have a ghost train for a den, and he could examine all the astonishing models and machinery without the slightest danger of nightmares. If only he could turn on the lights.

Grandma Cotton said that there must be a switch somewhere, and she struggled even on her hands and knees, gazing into every crevice, but found nothing. Then Tommy Cotton had an idea. He realised

that Mr Flanagan was extremely tall, and Grandma Cotton was very small. So, one night after the ghost train had closed, he set off with a ladder and Mickey Niff, to look upwards instead of downwards.

Mickey Niff carried one end of the ladder and a torch. He walked behind Tommy Cotton, so that he could look uncomfortably doubtful on the way. He thought that a den in the ghost train was a fantastic idea for tomorrow or for whatever time that was not called "now".

"There might not be a switch," he remarked as they walked nearer and nearer to the fairground. "There might be a button to press instead."

They crossed the road and walked on, saying nothing more until they turned the corner. There, in front of them, rose the dark shape of the fairground. The music had stopped. Everywhere was deserted. Tommy Cotton leaned the ladder against the frontage of the ghost train. Mickey Niff shone the torch above his head. Together they began to search for the light switch.

"Perhaps there isn't one at all," Mickey Niff said, almost hopefully. But Tommy Cotton took no notice.

"There must be," he said. "Mr Flanagan would need to see everything." He grinned and added, excitedly, "We'll see everything too. Shine the torch up here, Mickey Niff."

Tommy Cotton climbed to the last rung and stretched as high as he could. "I can just reach the top," he called down.

Tommy Cotton searched every inch of the dark wall. He wondered if he would ever find the switch for the lights, and if he really would be able to make a den there with Mickey Niff, their own special, secret place. He reached out in all directions, as though he might find a hidden trapdoor. But there were only the cold, hard bricks of the wall. He climbed down slowly, and moved the ladder to a different place.

"There must a switch somewhere," he said, crossly. Mickey Niff looked concerned.

"There's a crowd of weird things at the other side of that wall," he said, whispering, as though the weird things might be easily disturbed. The fairground seemed an eerie place too. "Why don't we come back when it isn't dark?"

"The ghost train isn't closed when it isn't dark," Tommy Cotton reminded him.

After a while, Tommy Cotton had to admit, there was no clue to tell them where the switch might be. He stood on the ground, leaning against the ladder, looking gloomy.

"If we don't find the switch, we'll never be able to explore the ghost train," he said, "or make our own den."

"Perhaps Mr Flanagan only has a torch," Mickey Niff said.

"He couldn't only have a torch," Tommy Cotton argued. "He'd need two hands to set up all those fantastic illusions and machinery. There must be lights in there."

"Perhaps the switch is on the other side of the doors," Mickey Niff suggested, with a shiver. "There isn't a way through the doors unless we ride in a truck, and then we'd only be carried away in the dark."

Tommy Cotton sighed.

"We'll have just one more look around," he said. He pressed both hands flat against the wall, feeling everywhere. Then, suddenly, he shouted,

"There's something here! Shine the torch, Mickey Niff!"   In the beam of light, they could see that there was a very small switch, painted black to match the wall, and pointing upwards.

Tommy Cotton shivered with excitement while Mickey Niff stared, wide-eyed.

"Now we can go inside," Tommy Cotton said, whispering, "and look at everything properly." His eyes shone in the dark, and he reached out and pressed down the switch. Click! There was only the faintest sound. "Come on!" he said, excitedly.

He reached out to press the switch that set the truck in motion, and jumped inside, quickly pulling Mickey Niff in after him.

Slowly, they glided to the huge, black doors, which swung open, suddenly. They hung on to the rail in front of them, breathless with excitement.

They looked around, staring in amazement. They gasped, spellbound. Filled with light, the ghost train was a changed, magical place, the most wonderful place they had ever seen.

The truck moved forward, gliding slowly, making no sound. Nothing moved, only the truck, as though the figures were frozen in the light.

The witches were still, as though a treacherous spell had turned them into stone. They crouched, fantastic and grotesque, fastened like prisoners in the glittering spiders' webs. Gruesome and ugly in the darkness and the shadows of the day, now under the light, the witches were quite magnificent.

The fearful skeletons sprawled innocent and lifeless on the ground like old, forgotten toys, but seemed to smile. And one by one, the ghosts had fallen soft as snow to settle near the silent witches' shoes, making no sound.

The truck moved on and on. The bats hung like the leaves, pinned on the silvery branches of the trees. The angry bog that in the daytime swirled and churned was still, placid as milk, the dreaded Boglins and the nasty Pondites deep inside, like children

put to bed. And still, the truck moved on
the twisting, turning rail, as though the
ghost train was a different, unknown place,
an undiscovered planet, even the moon.

"Is this really going to be our den?"
asked Mickey Niff, his voice an astonished
whisper. Tommy Cotton glowed.

"It really is," he answered slowly,
whispering too. They stared back at the
red-eyed, hairy ghouls, and at the gremlins
with their curious pointed ears, and
withered skin. But nothing moved, except

the truck that glided by without a sound, and everything was cast in silver under spiders' webs and light. The truck turned slowly round, encircling the dark pond, and entering a crevice in the rocks.

A cloak, beetle-black and shining, and half-hidden, fluttered in a sudden unexpected breeze. The wind grew stronger, stirring the sleeping, cloud-like ghosts, and tearing the festooned webs that dropped and hung in shreds. The wind made ripples on the pond, like wrinkles on an ugly witch's face. Ahead, the ghost-train doors were opening and letting in the night time fairground air.

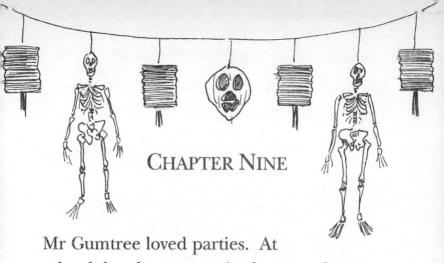

CHAPTER NINE

Mr Gumtree loved parties. At
school, he always organised a party for
Hallowe'en. He asked the children in
Tommy Cotton's class to provide the food.

"Will you bring plenty of jam tarts,
Tommy Cotton?" he asked, hopefully.
Tommy Cotton said that he would, and
asked,

"Is this a fancy dress party?"

"Of course," Mr Gumtree said, smiling,
"and there's a prize, for the best costume."
He read from the list on his desk.

"Toffee apples?" Several hands shot up
in front of him. Mr Gumtree wrote down
names, then glancing around again asked,
"Spicy sausages? Pumpkin pie?"

Soon everyone had agreed to bring a contribution to the buffet. The rest of the school were bringing pumpkins and turnips, and candles and balloons. The school band was providing the music.

On the day of the party, Tommy Cotton's class helped Mr Gumtree to decorate the school hall. All the children went home early to dress up. The musical instruments were arranged in a corner, and the music stands were decorated with hundreds of coloured balloons.

Everywhere, there were the empty
shells of pumpkins and turnips,
holding the candles that waited to be lit.
Grandma Cotton was going to the party too,
to help serve the food.

That evening, the school band were
playing catchy tunes as the first children
arrived. The candles inside the pumpkins
were lit, casting a wonderful warm glow
everywhere, and making flickering shadows.
Everyone came wearing spooky fancy dress.

The prize was tickets for the pantomine at Christmas, so most people tried very hard to be the best dressed person there.

'This is going to be a marvellous party," Tommy Cotton said, looking around. He could hardly recognise anyone, because most people were wearing masks. There were witches wearing tall hats and carrying broomsticks, talking and laughing with ghosts. Tommy Cotton and Mickey Niff were dressed as skeletons.

Mickey Niff said, "I don't think we"ll win the prize," because several other people were skeletons too.

Soon, the party was in full swing. No one knew just then that there would be an unexpected visitor to the party, and this was the way it happened.

Mr Flanagan had been working on his plan to scare Grandma Cotton out of her wits. He had used all his imagination to make the most horrendous witch of all. He needed to use Mrs Flanagan as a base model so that his very scary witch could chase Grandma Cotton up hill and down dale, or at least, halfway across the town. His mechanised ghost-train witches would not move outside the ghost train. Only Mrs Flanagan had real legs that could run around. If only Mr Flanagan could really scare Grandma Cotton, he would not be in such a dreadful state and feel such a failure.

"This is your most important assignment," Mr Flanagan told Mrs Flanagan, who was as thin as a poker, too. Mrs Flanagan was to carry her broomstick and her screeching, green-eyed cat to add to the effects. She was very excited.

"Shall I wear the cockroach brooch?" she asked, proudly.

"Of course," Mr Flanagan told her. "I bought it for you to wear on special occasions."

Often, the most clever people make magnificent plans, taking weeks, and amazingly, one tiny mistake can ruin everything. Hallowe'en was the exact night Mr Flanagan chose to frighten Grandma Cotton out of her wits.

As soon as he had drawn up plans, he had simply said, "We'll scare Grandma Cotton next Thursday," thinking that next Thursday was a perfectly ordinary day. He might just as well have said next Tuesday, or next Saturday. He had been so intent on making Mrs Flanagan into the spookiest witch of all time, that he completely forgot Hallowe'en, the very night that he of all people, usually celebrated in style.

That night, Mr and Mrs Flanagan skulked bent-kneed out of their house, with Mrs

Flanagan's blackest of black
cats prowling after them.
They soon arrived, unseen,
at the back of the ghost
train. Mr Flanagan
unlocked a
secret
door and
pouff! They were both inside.

Mrs Flanagan began to dress in
gruesome and grisly clothes. She put on a
long, black dress and spiky, pointed shoes.
Then, she wore a shiny, beetle-black cloak,
with Mr Flanagan's favourite grisly garnishes.
There was no doubt that Mrs Flanagan's
outfit and embellishments were the work of
a genius! Mrs Flanagan was changed into
the most sensational witch ever created, with
the complexion of a ploughed field, teeth
the shape of bent nails, and a cackle that
would shatter glass. Mr Flanagan stood back
in the wispy, grey shadows to see the effect.

"Stupendous!" he said, with a gasp of happiness, and wringing his hands together.

At that moment, only inches away, Grandma Cotton was rummaging in her knitting bag for a lost ball of wool, before making her way to the party. She had no idea of the impending danger. She could not even guess that soon she

might be running as fast as her legs could carry her, away from a terrifying witch that might chase her for miles, a witch that seemed to have come to life and escaped from Mr Flanagan's famous ghost train. In the darkest of black darkness, Mrs Flanagan sidled towards the exit door and prepared to terrify.

Slowly, the dark, dismal door of the ghost train swung open to reveal the dreaded Mrs Flanagan, in all her ghastly finery!

Grandma Cotton looked up. She *almost* had the fright of her life, but remembered in the nick of time that of course, it was Hallowe'en. She stared at the witch-like Mrs Flanagan. Then, amazingly cheerful in circumstances which would have chilled any other person to the bone, Grandma Cotton said, "Well, you do look fancy!" because she thought there was a good chance that this was Harry Pickup, from Mr Gumtree's class, dawdling or looking for hot dogs, even though the fairground had just closed. Mrs Flanagan was a small, wizened creature, only the size of Harry Pickup, under the hat. So Grandma Cotton added, "Do hurry along to school or you'll miss the party! Looking like that, you could easily win the tickets for the pantomine. You'll be the best dressed witch there!"

Mrs Flanagan pricked up her bat ears and didn't need telling twice. She had never been to a party or a pantomine in her life and she wasn't going to miss the chance. The school, did she hear Grandma Cotton say? She set off to Tommy Cotton's school, at a creaking, cracking pace.

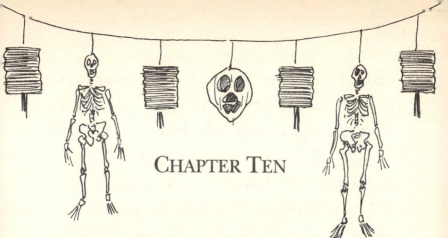

CHAPTER TEN

Mrs Flanagan whizzed into school, cloak flying. She arrived in full splendour, clutching a green-eyed cat which was alive and flustered, and a broomstick. Mr Flanagan had trimmed her tall, pointed hat with a real toad to match her complexion. The toad reclined on the brim. Tommy Cotton and Mickey Niff saw Mrs Flanagan arrive.

"That's an amazing costume," Tommy Cotton gasped.

"I knew we wouldn't win," Mickey Niff murmured, staring. "Who can that be?" Tommy Cotton was fascinated. They watched Mrs Flanagan in astonishment.

This was definitely Mrs Flanagan's kind

of party. Everything she saw made her feel
excited and the music from the school band
made her feet joggle. Mrs Flanagan began
to have the time of her life. She had never
danced before, but was quick at learning.
The only nuisance was that when she
danced really madly, the tall, pointed hat
bounced onto the floor and the toad
hopped off. Before long, she had flung the
hat onto the nearest chair where she had
left the green-eyed black cat. The cat was
sound asleep next to the broomstick she
had exchanged for a toffee apple.

Of course, no one had the slightest idea
that Mrs Flanagan was at the party. No one
knew *anyone* that night!

Mrs Flanagan bit sharply into the toffee
apple. The toffee was rock-hard against the
dreadful and ghastly-coloured teeth.

But Mr Flanagan had not expected that
Mrs Flanagan would be introduced to the
delights of the toffee apple. One by one,
the terrible teeth snapped into pieces, and
were missing.

The children arrived at the buffet table like seagulls at a picnic. There was such a crush at the tables in the dining hall. Grandma Cotton filled glasses with a dark red drink she called Witches' Brew. Mr Gumtree saved one or two jam tarts behind a curtain on the window ledge. In hardly any time at all, there were only crumbs and a tablecloth.

Back in the school hall, the Headmaster, who was tall and thin, although not at all like Mr Flanagan in any other way, stood next to Mr Gumtree, who was quite round, like an orange. They scanned the fancy dress costumes. Tommy Cotton and Mickey Niff lined up for the judging of the competition. Of course, everyone was hidden under a mask, although Tommy Cotton could always tell which skeleton was Mickey Niff.

He told Mickey Niff, "We should've come as spiders. There are no spider outfits tonight. Spiders would've been easy." Mr Gumtree, who wore his skipping rope smile, was only vaguely reminded of Mr Flanagan's ghost train in spite of all the skeletons and witches. He stood in the centre of the hall with the Headmaster.

"I can see you've all made tremendous efforts to win the prize," he said, politely really, considering that most of the masks had come from the newsagent's shop.

Mrs Flanagan had thrown off her shoes and had danced away the warts. She had felt too hot, and had flung down the beetle-black cloak, too.

"Now then, please move slowly around the hall so that we can see everyone properly." Mr Gumtree called out. Everyone made a huge circle. The Headmaster peered closely at all the fancy dress costumes and decided that he liked the witches more than he liked the skeletons.

"Would all the witches make a smaller

circle in the centre," the Headmaster added, cheerfully.

"I told you we wouldn't win," Mickey Niff said, disappointedly.

"I didn't expect we would either," Tommy Cotton agreed. "Anyway, there's a conjuror waiting to come in."

Harry Pickup was dressed as a witch too. He had wrapped himself in the glittering black and gold cape he had found in his auntie's attic. He was carrying Mrs Flanagan's cat, because he had found it lost and howling near the dustbins. For weeks, Harry Pickup had collected old pieces of wool and glued them to the edge of the tall and pointed hat he had made out of shiny black card.

But, by mistake, Mrs Flanagan was wearing Harry Pickup's hat and he was wearing hers, although the toad puzzled him. Mrs Flanagan's warts littered the floor. Harry Pickup fixed them onto himself instead with glue.

The spiders he had made with paper and black shoelaces, were not at all convincing as they lay on the kitchen table on a sunny Saturday morning. Harry Pickup fixed them together anyway. Attached to elastic bands, they ran and bounced in all directions. That night, he wore them like a scarf. In the shadowy dim candlelight of the school hall, his spiders were terrifyingly real.

Harry Pickup had ridden on Mr Flanagan's ghost train more than once and was an impressionable child.

He remembered
the curved and
twisted fingernails.
He had painted his
face light green, and
had fixed on a crooked
nose and his own warts
made of walnuts. The
cat added a realistic
touch, and the hat was
stupendous. Also, Harry Pickup was
not eating a toffee apple.

"Toffee apples rot your teeth," Mrs Pickup
always said.

Harry Pickup began to look more and
more like Mrs Flanagan, while Mrs Flanagan
was losing all the witchiness that was not her
very own.

"I wonder who that witch can be?" Mickey
Niff sighed, looking envious, and gazing at the
horrible witch at the other side of the room.
But he was not looking at Mrs Flanagan!

Everyone began to notice Harry Pickup's efforts, although of course, no one knew that the efforts belonged to Harry Pickup.

Mr Gumtree signalled for the band to stop playing. There was a drum roll.

The Headmaster stepped forward and made an announcement.

"This is tonight's winner of the pantomime tickets," he said, happily, handing the envelope with the precious tickets inside to Harry Pickup. "Would you like to tell us who you really are?"

While Harry Pickup was explaining
that he was Harry Pickup, Mrs Flanagan
decided to behave like a real witch. She
stamped her feet on the floor in a terrible
temper and the sound of her nasty cackle
ripped through the school like splintering
glass. In a puff of smoke, Mrs Flanagan
disappeared into the night.

It was extraordinary that even later that night, Mr Flanagan still had not remembered that it was Hallowe'en. He waited for hours and hours for the frightful chase to begin. What could have happened? Where was Mrs Flanagan? Why was Grandma Cotton not running as fast as her legs could carry her, away from the best witch he had ever made? He waited for a long, long time.

Mr Flanagan waited until the Hallowe'en party was over. The children were on their way home, still wearing their costumes.

Suddenly, in the distance, Mr Flanagan saw a strange shape, that came nearer and nearer. He peered more closely. To his horror, he saw that the strange shape was a skeleton! Behind the skeleton was a pale and misty ghost! Where had they come from? The ghost train? Had his terrible inventions come alive? Had they escaped to haunt him?

He saw witches mingling with the ghosts, coming one after the other, in twos and threes, and crowds, laughing together in the night air. They moved closer and closer, hundreds more following, coming more quickly. They were coming to exactly that spot on which he was standing, casting shadows in the moonlight.

There were ghosts and witches everywhere. Wherever he looked around him, he saw spiders and toads and skeletons.

Mr Flanagan's heart began to pound. He turned and began to walk quickly away. But he could hear them following him.

He began to run, faster and faster, in the
dark blackness of the night.

The bones of the skeletons rattled in his
ears. He thought he saw bats fly in the sky.
The black cloaks of the witches darkened
the sky, shutting out the moonlight and the
stars.

Mr Flanagan ran and ran. His long,
thin legs ran spider-fast through the town.
Every terrible creature and horrible thing
was chasing him. He shivered and shook
with a terrible fright into the blackest of
black darkness.

Mr Gumtree did not need to write to the Town Council to ask for the Ghost Train to be closed down. One day, Mr Flanagan closed down the Ghost Train himself.

The Ghost Train became an excellent Museum of Horrible Things.

Mr Flanagan joined Mr Gumtree's Model Railway Society and was interested in all other kinds of trains.

Mrs Flanagan applied complexion cream.

Grandma and Tommy Cotton, and Mickey Niff stayed the same.

THE DARK AT THE FOOT OF THE STAIRS

Eileen Moore

Illustrated by Moira Kemp

Spiders! Like them or loathe them – every house has got them. But Tommy Cotton's spider is rather unusual…

It's much much bigger than your average creepy-crawly, and it could be lurking about anywhere…

It likes bananas, and frogs, and the dark at the foot of Grandma Cotton's stairs…

h HODDER **Also by Hodder Children's books**

THE WORM AND THE TOFFEE-NOSED PRINCESS

Eva Ibbotson

Illustrated by Russell Ayto

Sometimes a snooty princess needs teaching a lesson. A hungry, hairy worm should do the trick! And anyone who dares to annoy the Frid Monster is just looking for trouble.

Read on, and enjoy a magical monster experience in Eva Ibbotson's creepy monster collection…

A DOG OF MY OWN

Alan Brown

All Tom ever wanted was a dog of his own. And when trouble strikes, his dream comes true and George bounds into his life.

This wild puppy arrives just when Tom needs him the most, and Tom will do anything to keep him...

THE HAUNTED SUITCASE

Colin Thompson

In a small seaside town stands a tall dark house. Every brick, from the steepest chimneys, to the deepest cellar, is dripping with memories and ghosts.

The Haunted Suitcase is churning out every lost sock in the world. The old sea dog, Dogbreath Magroo, has spent centuries spreading hairs. And the Plughole Fairy is causing chaos in the bathroom.

This is no ordinary haunted house…

hODDER **Also by Hodder Children's books**

CASTLE TWILIGHT AND OTHER STORIES

Colin Thompson

Castle Twilight sits hidden, brooding between cold mountains. Windows, like empty eyes, gaze down all-seeing on those who perpetually live in its shadow...

All manner of unsavoury, unsightly characters lurk here : Meddler and Leaky, two blind witches whose noses snout out everybody's business. Headache, the ugliest dog in the world. And Creepeasy, the butler with a serious attitude problem!

Welcome to Castle Twilight...

h **Also by Hodder Children's books**

SECRET FRIENDS

Elizabeth Laird

Rafaella doesn't find it easy to make friends. Her name sounds strange. Her ears stick out. She feels different from the others. And Lucy is the first to tease, the first to call her 'Earwig'.

Then a secret friendship starts – full of warmth and mystery...

SHAGGY GHOST STORIES

Shoo Rayner

Who is the ghostess with the mostess?
Why would a ghoul need to visit the doctor?
And are high spirits really just spooks on top
of a mountain?

This gaggle of ghoulish giggles guarantees to
keep you howling through the night – this is
a joke book with a difference?

ORDER FORM

0 340 64873 2	Dark at the Foot of the Stairs	£3.50	☐
0 340 68740 1	The Worm and the Toffee…	£3.50	☐
0 340 68658 8	A Dog of My Own	£3.50	☐
0 340 64849 X	The Haunted Suitcase…	£3.50	☐
0 340 64850 3	Castle Twilight	£3.50	☐
0 340 66473 8	Secret Friends	£3.50	☐
0 340 69013 5	Shaggy Ghost Stories	£3.50	☐

All Hodder Children's books are available at your local bookshop, or can be ordered direct from the publisher. Just tick the titles you would like and complete the details below. Prices and availability are subject to change without prior notice.

Please enclose a cheque or postal order made payable to Bookpoint Ltd and send to Hodder Children's Books, 39 Milton Park, Abingdon, OXON OX14 4TD, UK. Or email at: orders@bookpoint.co.uk

If you would prefer to pay by credit card, our call centre team would be delighted to take your order by phone. Our direct line 01235 400414 (9am-6pm Monday to Saturday). Alternatively you can fax on 01235 400454.

Title		First Name		Surname	
Address					
Daytime Tel				Postcode	